Aesop's
FABLES

To Alessia, Arianna, Giada, Olivia and in loving memory of Sophie W. FT

For John Welch 1926-2009. A wise and much missed friend. FMW

First published in Great Britain in 2010 by Andersen Press Ltd.,

20 Vauxhall Bridge Road, London SW1V 2SA.

Published in Australia by Random House Australia Pty.,

Level 3, 100 Pacific Highway, North Sydney, NSW 2060.

Text copyright © Fiona Waters, 2010. Illustration copyright © Fulvio Testa, 2010

The rights of Fiona Waters and Fulvio Testa to be identified as the

author and illustrator of this work have been asserted by them

in accordance with the Copyright, Designs and Patents Act, 1988.

All rights reserved. Colour separated in Switzerland by Photolitho AG, Zürich.

Printed and bound in China by Toppan Leefung.

Fulvio Testa has used pen and ink with watercolour in this book.

10   9   8   7   6   5   4   3   2   1

British Library Cataloguing in Publication Data available.

ISBN 978 1 84939 049 1

This book has been printed on acid-free paper

FULVIO TESTA

Aesop's FABLES

Retold by FIONA WATERS

ANDERSEN PRESS

CONTENTS

THE GOAT AND THE WOLF ~ 6

THE BULL AND THE GOATS ~ 8

THE WOLF AND THE HERON ~ 10

THE FOX AND THE GOAT ~ 12

THE FOX AND THE CROW ~ 14

THE LION AND THE MOUSE ~ 16

THE TOWN MOUSE AND THE COUNTRY MOUSE ~ 18

THE OX AND THE FROG ~ 20

THE FOX AND THE ROSE BUSH ~ 22

THE ANT AND THE CICADA ~ 24

THE GNAT AND THE LION ~ 26

THE FOX AND THE STORK ~ 28

THE HARE AND THE TORTOISE ~ 30

THE TORTOISE AND THE EAGLE ~ 32

THE CAT AND THE MICE ~ 34

THE LION AND THE ASS ~ 36

THE ASS IN THE LION'S SKIN ~ 38

ANOTHER ASS IN THE LION'S SKIN ~ 40

THE ASS AND THE DOG ~ 42

THE CRAB AND HIS MOTHER ~ 44

THE CAGED BIRD AND THE BAT ~ 46

THE HARES AND THE FROGS ~ 48

THE WOLF AND HIS SHADOW ~ 50

THE OLD LION ~ 52

THE LION AND THE BOAR ~ 54

THE LION AND THE HARE ~ 56

THE SWOLLEN FOX ~ 58

THE BOY WHO CRIED WOLF ~ 60

THE LION AND THE STAG ~ 62

THE WILD BOAR AND THE FOX ~ 64

THE DOG AND THE EGG ~ 66

THE LION AND THE FROG ~ 68

THE FOX AND THE WOODCUTTER ~ 70

THE HUNTING DOG, THE LION AND THE FOX ~ 72

THE ANT AND THE DOVE ~ 74

THE FOX AND THE ACTOR'S MASK ~ 76

THE FOX AND THE GRAPES ~ 78

THE MONKEY AS KING ~ 80

THE FOX AND THE MONKEY ~ 82

THE FOX WITHOUT A TAIL ~ 84

THE LION, THE BEAR AND THE FOX ~ 86

THE LION, THE FOX AND THE DONKEY ~ 88

THE ASS, THE FOX AND THE LION ~ 90

THE MAN AND THE LION ~ 92

THE LION, THE WOLF AND THE FOX ~ 94

THE WOLF AND THE LAMB ~ 96

THE WOLF AND THE LION ~ 98

THE GOATHERD AND THE WILD GOATS ~ 100

THE TAME ASS AND THE WILD ASS ~ 102

THE ASS CARRYING THE STATUE ~ 104

THE ASS AND THE WOLF ~ 106

THE DOG AND THE WOLF ~ 108

THE DOG AND THE SHADOW ~ 110

THE PIG AND THE SHEEP ~ 112

THE FOX AND THE CICADA ~ 114

THE GNAT AND THE BULL ~ 116

THE LION, JUPITER AND THE ELEPHANT ~ 118

THE DOG, THE COCK AND THE FOX ~ 120

THE ASS AND THE SHEPHERD ~ 122

THE HARE AND THE HOUND ~ 124

ABOUT AESOP ~ 126

ABOUT FULVIO TESTA AND FIONA WATERS ~ 128

The Goat and the Wolf

The sun was shining and the little goat was enjoying the warmth on his coat. Everywhere he looked there were tussocks of even more delicious grass just beyond the last, and before he knew it he had strayed quite far from the rest of his flock. Suddenly, he heard a terrible sound that stopped him in his tracks. It was the snarl of a wolf. Slowly the little goat turned round, his legs trembling, and sure enough, there stood a large and shaggy wolf. He was smiling in a most unpleasant way, revealing lots of very sharp teeth.

But little goats are often a lot smarter than shaggy old wolves so, thinking quickly, the little goat took a couple of steps forward and said, "I know, Wolf, that you are planning to have me for your lunch, but perhaps you would grant me one last wish. Please would you play your flute so I can have one last dance?"

The wolf was quite happy to play a merry tune before his lunch, so he whipped out his flute. The little goat kicked up his heels and danced as if he didn't have a care in the world. Faster and faster, and louder and louder the wolf played, and suddenly the dogs guarding the flock, who had been dozing in the shade, came racing up, barking loudly. The wolf dropped the flute, turned tail and fled back up the path and was out of sight in seconds, muttering as he went, "Serves me right. I should not have allowed myself to be distracted from catching my lunch."

ALWAYS ATTEND TO THE MATTER IN HAND OR YOU MAY LOSE EVERYTHING.

The Bull and the Goats

A big old bull was being chased by a lion. Desperate to escape, the bull charged into a cave where he thought he might be safe until the lion became bored and went off somewhere else to look for his next meal. The lion paced up and down outside, peering into the dark of the cave. But what the bull had not realised was that the cave was full of wild goats. Needless to say, the goats were not at all happy at having such a great big beast in their midst, so they all began butting the bull with their horns, which were very sharp. The bull just stood there, even though the goats were really beginning to hurt him.

"I am not as afraid of you hurting me, goats," he bellowed, "as I am of being eaten by that lion out there, so I will just have to put up with your very sharp horns."

IF YOU ARE MORE AFRAID OF SOMEONE BIGGER, YOU WILL OFTEN PUT UP WITH HURT FROM SOMEONE SMALLER.

The Wolf and the Heron

A greedy old wolf caught a huge fish and in his haste to gobble it all up, he managed to get a large bone caught in his throat. It was very painful and he couldn't swallow properly. He became very worried about ever being able to eat again, which wouldn't have suited him at all, of course.

He wandered about crossly, but there didn't seem to be anyone who could help him, so he was getting more and more anxious. And then he saw a heron, who had a very long beak.

"Aha," he thought. "Just the person."

He sidled up to the heron and attempted to smile. "Dear Heron, I wonder if you could possibly help me. I have a huge bone caught in my throat and if it isn't taken out soon, I shall starve to death," he said, trying to look pathetic. "I shall, of course, reward you handsomely."

So the trusting heron put his head down the wolf's very large throat and carefully drew out the bone.

"There you are, it is out," said the heron. "Now, where is my reward?"

The wolf grinned nastily. "Your reward is that I didn't bite your head off while it was down my throat. What more do you want?" and he sloped off without a backward glance.

IF YOU ARE KIND TO UNTRUSTWORTHY PEOPLE YOU WILL RARELY BE THANKED.

The Fox and the Goat

The cunning fox was out for a stroll one day, when he had the great misfortune to fall down a well. He tried jumping back out again, but the sides were too deep, so he was well and truly stuck. He sat there for a very long time, desperately thinking of a way to get out. He had just about given up hope, when a head appeared over the edge of the well. It was a goat.

"Hello," said the goat. "What are you doing down there?"

The fox realised he could be saved by the trusting goat. He looked up and said, "My dear friend, I am enjoying this marvellously pure water. I have never tasted anything quite like it before."

As it happened, the goat was very thirsty so without further ado he jumped down beside the fox and drank his fill.

"It is indeed very refreshing water. Thank you for sharing it with me," said the goat. "Now how do we get out of here?"

The fox pretended to think for a while and then said, "I have an idea. Why don't you stand on your hind legs and lean up against the side of the well? Then I can clamber up over your shoulders, and then step onto your horns and I should just about make it."

The goat did as the fox suggested and in no time at all the fox was out of the well and walking away.

The goat called loudly after him, "My turn now. How do I get out?"

But the fox just laughed and strolled off, calling over his shoulder, "If you had as much sense in your head as you have hairs in your beard, you wouldn't have jumped into the well in the first place without thinking about how to get out again."

LOOK BEFORE YOU LEAP.

The Fox and the Crow

A crow was wheeling through the sky, when she spotted a piece of cheese dropped by a passing shepherd. She swooped down and pounced on it, and then flapped off to a nearby tree to eat her feast. But she had been seen by a wily fox who was determined to have the cheese for himself. He loped up to the tree and began praising the crow in the most extravagant manner.

"Mistress Crow, you are such a noble bird. Your plumage is so lustrous and your beak so sharp. I am sure you must be the Queen of all Birds."

The crow puffed herself up and was very taken with all this flattery.

The fox continued, "I am sure the Queen of all Birds has a glorious singing voice, more beautiful than any other."

Now the crow, of course, did not have a beautiful voice at all, but she was determined to convince the fox that she was indeed the Queen of all Birds, so she opened her beak and gave a loud caw. Down dropped the piece of cheese and the fox gobbled it up immediately.

"If you really were the Queen of all Birds, I am sure you would have brains as well," he said as he ran off, leaving the furious crow to regret her foolishness.

FLATTERY IS THE MOST INSINCERE FORM OF PRAISE.

The Lion and the Mouse

A little mouse was running through a dark cave, when she most unfortunately ran over the mane of a sleeping lion. The lion was very grumpy at being woken up in such a way and flattened the little mouse with one swipe of his paw. He was about to pop her into his cavernous mouth when the mouse piped up, "Please don't eat me, oh great Lion! Let me go and perhaps one day I might be able to help you."

The lion roared with laughter at the impudence of the tiny mouse. "As if such an insignificant creature as you could possibly help such a great beast as myself," he said, but he let her go without harming her.

Now it happened that not very long afterwards, the great lion was captured by some hunters. They trussed him up with ropes and then went off to get a cart to carry him back to their village. The lion was furious and roared in anger. The sound echoed round the woods and the little mouse heard it as she lay in her warm nest. She recognised his voice and immediately ran to see what was wrong. She looked at him lying helpless on the ground and said, "I can help you, oh great Lion, if you will let me."

The lion just looked at her in disbelief.

"How can so tiny a creature possibly help me? As soon as the hunters come back, they will drag me off to their village and that will be the end of me."

"Do be quiet," said the mouse, "and let me get on with what I have to do." And she hopped up onto the mighty lion's great shoulders and began to gnaw away at the ropes that were tightly bound round his huge body. She gnawed and gnawed, and one by one the ropes sprang apart. Before long, the lion was standing upright again with strands of the broken ropes about his feet, looking humbly at the tiny mouse. "You see," she said with a twinkle in her eye, "even the mighty sometimes need the help of the most insignificant."

SOMETIMES EVEN THE STRONGEST PERSON NEEDS A WEAKER PERSON'S HELP.

The Town Mouse and the Country Mouse

One day a country mouse invited a town mouse to stay with him in the country. They had a pleasant time sitting by the river bank and talking, and then went to dine at the country mouse's humble home. The fare was simple - nuts and berries and husks of corn, which the country mouse had carefully gathered from the fields about his home. The town mouse was not impressed. "My dear fellow, this is very meagre food. Come to the town with me and see just what a fantastic spread I have to choose from."

The country mouse was rather upset by the town mouse's ingratitude, but he said nothing, and they made their way to the town. The town mouse suddenly dived through a hole in a wall and the country mouse slipped in quietly behind him. A long dusty passage opened out into a vast room.

"Now, quickly," said the town mouse, "come and help yourself to some really delicious food," and he darted up the long leg of a very high table. The country mouse scrambled up after him, and his eyes nearly popped out when he saw the feast laid out. There was a huge cheese, a bowl of rare nuts, shiny apples and figs, a fine freshly baked loaf and much, much more besides.

The country mouse didn't know where to start, and had just nibbled a small piece of the cheese, when the door to the room opened with a bang. The town mouse slipped down the table leg in a flash and scuttled into the dusty passage, almost before the country mouse had time to register what had happened.

"Scat, you filthy vermin!" and a huge human hand came looming down over the country mouse. With a squeak of terror, he hurtled down the table leg and flung himself after the town mouse.

His heart pounding, the country mouse said to his friend, "I am sorry, but I think for all the riches available in the town, I would rather have my simple, but very safe, way of life," and, murmuring his thanks, he scuttled back to his simple little home as fast as his legs could take him.

A SIMPLE BUT SAFE LIFE IS BETTER THAN A RICH BUT DANGEROUS ONE.

The Ox and the Frog

The frog was sitting on a stone in the middle of the pond, with his younger brothers and sisters all around him. Occasionally the frog's tongue darted out and he slurped up a passing dragonfly. He was very content. As he looked out over the meadow, a grazing ox came into sight.

"What a very big creature," gasped the frog's littlest sister.

"Do you really think so?" said the frog. "I can make myself just as big," and he puffed out his chest as far as possible.

"The ox is still bigger," said the littlest sister.

"Well, I shall make myself bigger still," boasted the silly frog. And he puffed and puffed, stretching his skin until it was tight as tight could be.

"The ox is still bigger," said the littlest sister in a tiny voice for she was afraid her big brother would be cross.

"I can make myself even bigger, I really can," yelled the cross frog. And he puffed and puffed until – with a loud bang – he burst! And that was the end of him.

NEVER TRY TO MAKE YOURSELF WHAT YOU ARE NOT.

The Fox and the Rose Bush

The fox decided to take a shortcut home. He leapt over a fence, but just as he was about to land on the other side, he realised he was going to fall onto a rose bush. He reached out a paw to stop himself, but he was too late and caught himself on a particularly sharp thorn.

"Ouch!" he yelled. "You might have saved me from such a painful landing. I needed your help," he said to the rose bush.

"Well, you made a very foolish mistake," retorted the rose bush. "Why should I not catch hold of you? That is what I am here to do - catch hold of people."

NEVER ASK SOMEONE TO HELP YOU, IF IT IS THEIR NATURE TO HURT RATHER THAN HELP.

The Ant and the Cicada

It was a bright winter's day and the ants were busy drying out their store of wheat, which had become rather wet after a long spell of rain. They were all bustling about busily laying the grains out in the sun to dry. Here and there they hurried, all working away together. A cicada came by and after watching the ants for a moment, she flew up to the biggest one. "Please give me something to eat. I am really starving," she pleaded.

The biggest ant stopped what he was doing just long enough to ask the cicada, "Why should we give you any of our precious food? What, may I ask, were you doing in the summer when we were all working so hard to gather this store of food for the winter?"

The cicada laughed contemptuously. "Well I was singing, of course. I didn't have time to bother about gathering food!"

The ant shook his head and turned to go back to work. "As you were too busy singing in the summer to make sure you had food stored up, you will just have to dance through the winter," and he turned his back on the lazy cicada.

YOU SHOULD NEVER DEPEND ON THE GENEROSITY OF OTHERS, IF YOU HAVE MADE NO PROVISION FOR YOURSELF.

The Gnat and the Lion

A boastful gnat flew up to a lion and buzzed irritatingly around his head.

"Of course, you don't frighten me one little bit," he sneered at the lion. "Your strength is nothing to me." The lion frowned, but said nothing. The gnat continued to flit about the lion's head.

"You can scratch with your claws and bite with your big teeth, but really, I am much stronger than you." The lion rose to his feet crossly, his tail swishing after the gnat.

"Hopeless," smirked the gnat. "Why don't we fight, and then you will see what I mean," and he darted down and bit the lion on the softest part of his nose. "Oww!" cried the lion and swiped at the gnat, but he missed, and scratched his poor wounded nose, making it even more painful. "See," cried the gnat, "I am victorious!" and he buzzed off triumphantly. But he wasn't looking where he was going, and he flew right into a spider's web, where he was soon totally entangled. In a second, the spider scuttled over and, with one gulp, she gobbled him up.

BE CAREFUL THAT YOU ARE NOT DEFEATED BY THE MOST INSIGNIFICANT ENEMY.

The Fox and the Stork

The stork unexpectedly met the fox just as she landed after a long journey across many lands. "Please allow me to give you dinner after your lengthy flight," said the fox, bowing graciously. The stork accepted the invitation gladly for as well as being exhausted, she was very thirsty.

The fox presented the weary bird with a dish of nourishing soup. But it was a flat dish and, try as she would, the poor stork could scoop nothing up from the plate, as her bill was too long and thin. The sly fox lapped up every last drop and sat back watching, with a rather nasty smile on his face. As the stork left, she invited the mean fox to join her the next day for dinner, and he accepted without a thought.

But when he arrived, the clever stork produced a delicious smelling soup, served in a narrow necked pitcher. As she slipped her bill in the pitcher and enjoyed her meal, the fox could do nothing, but scowl and reflect on his meanness.

DO AS YOU WOULD BE DONE BY.

The Hare and the Tortoise

The hare came lolloping across the field to where the tortoise was plodding along the road. "You are so slow!" the hare exclaimed. "Why don't you speed up?" But the tortoise just ignored him and continued down the road. "Slow coach!" taunted the hare. "I tell you what," said the tortoise slowly. "I bet I can win a race with you." "Nonsense!" said the hare. But he was so confident that he would win that he agreed to run the race. The fox started off the race, and away sped the hare and he was soon out of sight over the hill. The tortoise kept going, slowly and steadily. Down the road he went, one step after another, and eventually he, too, was over the hill. The hare, meanwhile, was so confident that he stopped for a rest and was playing a game, not looking at the road at all. Over the hill came the tortoise, one steady step at a time. Slowly, slowly he walked on without stopping until he overtook the hare, who was too busy to notice what was happening. On and on the tortoise walked, and in the distance he saw the fox standing at the finishing line. "Nearly there," said the tortoise to himself, and just kept walking. When he was a step away from the fox, he heard heavy breathing and the thump of feet on the road. As he crossed the finishing line, the tortoise turned slowly, slowly round and there was the hare running down the road for all he was worth, ears streaming out behind him. But the tortoise had won, fair and square.

SLOW AND STEADY WINS THE RACE.

The Tortoise and the Eagle

The tortoise was plodding along slowly, feeling more and more discontented with every lumbering step he took. He hated being so near to the ground and he hated being so slow. He craned his neck and looked enviously at the birds wheeling lazily in the sky. As he looked back down again, he spotted a huge eagle sitting on top of a nearby stone.

"Oh great Eagle, please teach me to fly!" he begged.

"Don't be ridiculous," snapped the eagle. "You are a lowly tortoise, and tortoises don't fly."

But the tortoise would not take no for an answer and kept pestering the eagle. The eagle pointed out again and again that it wasn't right for tortoises to fly. "You have no wings and all tortoises belong on the ground."

In the end the eagle could not put up with the tortoise's constant complaints and agreed to show him how to fly. Snatching him up in his talons, the eagle took off with the tortoise gripped firmly between his feet. Higher and higher they flew, and as they soared over the valley, the great eagle unleashed his talons and the tortoise dropped like a stone to the ground below. And that was the end of him.

YOU SHOULD ALWAYS LISTEN TO THOSE WHO KNOW BETTER.

The Cat and the Mice

A sneaky old cat heard that a certain house was quite overrun with mice, so she hied herself off there as fast as her paws would take her. There were indeed plenty of mice and the cat caught and ate them one by one. But the mice were not so silly and soon realised that they needed to put themselves out of harm's way from the sneaky cat. So all those remaining hid in the holes behind the skirting board and would not come out. The cat thought awhile and decided to play a trick on the mice. She clambered up the wall and hung herself from a peg, and kept very, very still, trying to pretend that she was dead.

But one of the mice peeped out of a hole and said, "We mice are not so silly, Cat. We know you are still alive, so we will just stay where we are for a while longer, until you get tired of hanging off that peg." And the cat did not catch another mouse in that house.

IF YOU ARE WISE, YOU WILL NOT BE FOOLED BY SOMEONE WHO HAS ONCE BEEN DANGEROUS TO YOU.

The Lion and the Ass

A foolish ass and a cunning lion set up in partnership and went out hunting together. They crept up very quietly to a cave, where they knew there was a herd of wild goats.

"Now, you go into the cave, and make a great deal of noise," said the lion to the ass. "And then the goats will all run outside in fright and I will catch them one by one."

So the foolish ass galloped into the cave, braying and stamping his hooves, and of course all the goats fled outside, where the lion managed to catch, each and every one. Once the cave was empty, the ass came out again and said to the lion, "Didn't I do well? I really scared them all!"

"My goodness me," laughed the lion, "if I hadn't known you were an ass, I would have been so frightened, I would have run away myself!"

IF YOU BOAST TO PEOPLE WHO KNOW YOU TOO WELL, YOU MUST EXPECT TO BE LAUGHED AT.

The Ass in the Lion's Skin

One day a foolish ass happened to find a lion's skin. "Hah hah," he said to himself, "now I shall have some fun! I shall pretend to be a lion and I can frighten people." And he did. He draped the lion's skin round his shoulders and pulled the head over his long ears. As soon as people saw him coming, they screamed and took to their heels as fast as possible. Animals ran away from him, too. He was delighted. Everywhere he went no one stayed to get in his way. He reared up and in his triumph, brayed loudly. But a passing fox heard the terrible noise and realised that this was no fierce lion but a miserable old ass. "Ah, you are not what you seem, Master Lion. You are just a foolish ass!" he said. And once all the animals saw what he really was, they all laughed at the ass in his lion's skin.

DO NOT PUT ON AIRS AND GRACES FOR AS SOON AS YOU OPEN YOUR MOUTH, YOU WILL BE FOUND OUT.

Another Ass in the Lion's Skin

Another ass found the lion's skin lying where the first ass had dropped it in shame. He, too, was all set to scare people, but his reign was cut short by a sudden gust of wind that blew the skin off his back and left him exposed as just another foolish ass. And this time all the people ran up and began to hit the ass with sticks and cudgels.

IF YOU ARE POOR, DO NOT TRY TO PRETEND TO BE RICH. YOU CANNOT MAKE YOURSELF WHAT YOU ARE NOT.

The Ass and the Dog

The road was long, and the ass and the dog, who were travelling together, were getting weary. They had seen nothing of interest at all, when suddenly the dog spied something lying on the road. It was a sealed packet. The dog broke the large seal on the packet and spread the papers out on the road. But he couldn't read, so he asked the ass to tell him what it was all about. The ass cleared his throat self importantly and began to read out loud. As it happened, it was all about fodder - grass and barley and hay and bran. This was of no interest to the dog who soon became restless and then thoroughly bored.

"My dear friend," the dog said eventually. "Please do skip all this tedious stuff about hay and grass and whatnot, find the bit about meat and bones. That will make much more interesting reading."

The ass looked all through the papers, right to the very last page, but there was nothing at all about meat and bones.

"Well," said the dog, yawning, "throw the packet away. It is of no interest whatsoever."

WHAT IS OF INTEREST TO ONE PERSON MAY BE VERY BORING TO ANOTHER.

The Crab and his Mother

The crab and his mother were walking along the beach. It was a clear day and they could see for miles over the sea.

The crab kept bumping into his mother.

"Please do not walk sideways like that," snapped his mother, waving her front claws. "You keep barging into me."

The crab was not aware that he was walking any differently to normal, so he apologised to his mother straight away and said, "Please do show me, Mother, how I should walk."

So his mother tried to show the crab how to walk, but she, too, kept going sideways and bumping into her son. And so she realised that she had been wrong to find fault with her child, when she could not walk straight herself.

CORRECT YOUR OWN FAULTS BEFORE FINDING FAULT WITH OTHERS.

The Caged Bird and the Bat

The small bird sat in a cage on a window ledge. All day long she was silent while the other birds in the garden were singing, but as soon as it grew dark, she would start to sing to herself. She did have the most glorious voice. One evening a bat was flying past the open window when he heard her. "I have passed this window many times," said the bat, "but I have never heard you sing before."

"Ah," said the little bird, "I only sing at night."

"But why is this?" asked the bat. "All the other birds sing during the day and sleep at night."

"Well," explained the bird, "it was while I was singing during the day that I was captured and put in this cage. So it taught me a lesson - never to sing during the day."

The bat was puzzled.

"But my dear little bird, surely it is too late for you to be so cautious? You are locked in the cage now. If you had been careful before, you might still be free today."

IT IS TOO LATE TO BE CAREFUL AFTER YOU HAVE LET THINGS GO WRONG.

The Hares and the Frogs

The hares were holding a meeting. They were all trembling and in a state of great distress.

"We are beset on all sides," said one.

"Everywhere we go there is danger," cried another.

"There is an eagle on top of the mountain over there. He will swoop down, and one of us will die," moaned another.

"The humans are out hunting with their great big dogs," shouted one of the younger hares. "What will we do to save ourselves?"

And gradually they all decided it would be better to end their lives themselves immediately, rather than sit waiting to meet a terrible end at the hands of eagles, humans or dogs. So they all ran down to the pond nearby, intending to leap in and drown themselves.

But there were lots and lots of frogs sitting round the pond, and when they heard the thump of the hares' feet they all leapt into the water with a mighty "Croak!" and hid themselves in the weeds at the bottom of the pond.

"Stop, stop!" cried one of the older hares, who was a little wiser than the rest.

"Don't jump, my friends. If these frogs are frightened of us, they must be even more timid than we are."

THERE ARE OFTEN PEOPLE WHO ARE IN A WORSE STATE THAN OURSELVES.

The Wolf and his Shadow

The wolf was running across a meadow just as the sun was getting low in the sky at the end of the day. As he ran, he noticed his shadow racing along the ground beside him. It was so long, and it was so big!

"Why, look how long I am," he boasted to himself. "And look how big I am! Why have I ever been afraid of a lion? I should be the King of the Beasts, not him," and on and on he went in a similar vein.

But he was so busy boasting to himself that he did not notice the very large lion, stalking behind him. With one mighty leap the lion pounced, and that was the end of the conceited wolf.

CONCEIT WILL ONLY BRING YOU TO A BAD END.

The Old Lion

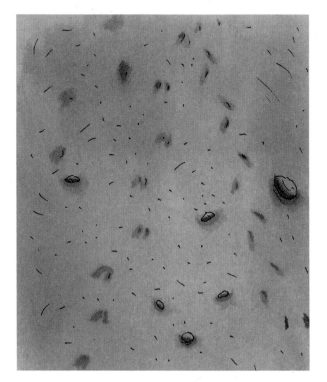

The lion was very old and not really able to hunt for his food any more. So he decided to use his cunning and get his meals to come to him. He found a cave which was warm and comfortable inside and also had a wide entrance. He lay down in this entrance and started to moan and groan. Before long a passing rabbit stopped to ask what was wrong. The wily lion answered that he was ill, so the poor foolish rabbit crept closer to see if there was anything she could do to help. In a flash, the lion gobbled her up. Many, many more animals were caught in this way, until one day it was a fox who stood some way off from the entrance to the cave. Now this was a clever fox and he looked very carefully at the lion before asking how he was.

"Oh, I am very unwell," said the lion. "Perhaps you might be able to help me. Why don't you come into my cave?" he added.

But the clever fox shook his head.

"I don't think so. I see lots of footprints going into your cave, but absolutely none coming out," and the clever fox walked away with a smile on his face.

ALWAYS LOOK CAREFULLY FOR DANGER SIGNALS BEFORE YOU ACT.

The Lion and the Boar

It was a very hot day and the sun was blazing down. The lion was looking forward to a deep, long drink as he padded slowly towards the pool. So, too, was the boar as he trotted towards the same pool. They both arrived at exactly the same time. They immediately began squabbling fiercely over who was there first and who had the most right to drink. And, of course, squabbling led to fighting and they were soon rolling around on the dusty ground, oblivious to anything other than their wish to defeat each other. But, as they paused for breath, in the same instant they both saw a most unwelcome sight. Wheeling in the sky and sitting on the rocks and in the trees were several vultures.

"These horrid birds are waiting to eat whichever one of us loses this battle," grumbled the lion quietly.

"Well, we shan't let that happen, shall we?" snorted the boar, and they both stopped quarrelling immediately and shared the pool, one at each side. They both drank their fill and walked away quite contented. The hungry vultures all flew away, screeching crossly to each other.

IN THE FACE OF MUTUAL ENEMIES, IT IS BETTER TO RECONCILE YOUR DIFFERENCES.

The Lion and the Hare

The lion was hungry and looking for something to eat when, by great good fortune, he came across a hare, fast asleep in the grass. Just as he was about to settle down for a good feast, a large stag came over the hill.

"Hah!" said the lion. "Why should I settle for this skinny hare, when I could have that whole stag all to myself?" And so he leapt up and ran after the stag, leaving the hare still fast asleep.

But the stag was fleet of foot and, although the lion ran as fast as he could, he was unable to get near, never mind actually catch him. Up and down they ran, round about, in and out, but the lion just could not overtake the stag. So puffing and panting, he sidled back to where he had left the hare. But when he reached the spot, the hare had disappeared too, so there was nothing left for his meal.

"Oh dear," grumbled the lion, "if only I had been content with the small hare, I would at least have had something to eat. Now I am exhausted and I have nothing!"

A BIRD IN THE HAND IS WORTH TWO IN THE BUSH.

The Swollen Fox

The fox was starving and just didn't know where his next meal was coming from. He ran hither and thither, desperately trying to find something he could eat. Suddenly he stopped dead in his tracks. There was a delicious smell coming from somewhere! He sniffed and sniffed. Where was it? His keen nose to the ground, he snuffled and sniffed and yes, there it was, a definite trail. It led right up to an old hollow tree and there, hidden carefully by a passing shepherd, the fox found a great quantity of bread and meat. The ravenous animal didn't wait. He slipped into the hollow tree and ate and ate until his skin was tight as a drum and he could not have eaten another scrap. He curled up contentedly and went to sleep. When he awoke a few hours later, he nibbled on a piece of bread, but, truth to tell, he was still so full he didn't really need it. Stretching, he rose slowly and went to climb out of the hollow tree. But he couldn't. His stomach was so full, he could not squeeze out of the opening, no matter how hard he tried. He pushed and pushed, and went this way and that, but still his big stomach was in the way. How on earth was he going to escape? He howled mournfully, but there was no getting away from it - he was stuck.

After a long while, another fox came by and when he heard what the problem was, he just laughed. "Serves you right for being so greedy. You will just have to stay there until you shrink back to your normal size," and the second fox went off, chuckling to himself.

Just before he slipped out of sight, he called back over his shoulder, "I hope you get thin enough to escape before the shepherd comes back. I don't suppose he will be very happy, when he finds out that you have eaten his supper!"

IF YOU TAKE YOUR TIME, YOU CAN SOLVE MOST PROBLEMS.

The Boy who cried Wolf

There was once a young shepherd boy who was always playing tricks on the other villagers. He would take his sheep to the furthest distant field and then dash back to the village, crying, "Help me, help me! A huge wolf is attacking my sheep!" and all the kindly villagers would stop whatever they were doing and run as fast as they could to chase the wolf away. But, of course, when they reached the flock, there was no wolf, only the silly shepherd boy rolling about with laughter.

"If only you could see your faces," he would shout. "I tricked you!" And the cross villagers would make their way back to the village to finish whatever they had been doing before being so rudely interrupted.

Two or three times the foolish boy played this trick, and on each occasion the helpful villagers would leave what they were doing, only to find that it was all a terrible waste of their time.

And then one day, two very large wolves really did come down from the hills and begin to attack the boy's sheep. He ran as fast as he had ever run, straight back to the village and called out, "Help me, help me! Two huge wolves are attacking my sheep!" But this time not a single person came rushing out of the village.

"Oh please, do help me! There really are two great wolves attacking my sheep!" the boy shouted in a desperate voice. But still no one came out.

"All my sheep are being eaten, what can I do alone?" the boy cried, tears running down his face.

The butcher came slowly out of his shop.

"Go away, boy, we are not going to be tricked by you again," he said crossly.

"But there really are wolves attacking my sheep," said the boy in despair.

"Deal with it yourself," said the butcher. "We are all too busy," and he turned and went back into his shop.

The boy turned away sadly and by the time he reached his flock again, he found that the wolves had eaten every single one of them.

IF YOU MAKE A HABIT OF TELLING LIES, YOU WILL NOT BE BELIEVED, EVEN WHEN YOU ARE TELLING THE TRUTH.

The Lion and the Stag

The stag was drinking at a pool one day and, once his thirst was quenched, he caught sight of his reflection in the water.

"My, what very fine antlers I have," he thought to himself proudly, and he turned this way and that, so he might admire himself even more. But then he saw his long thin legs.

"Oh dear," he grumbled, "those thin legs are not very impressive. I wish they were better looking." And he would have gone on in this foolish manner had he not seen another reflection in the water. It was a lion!

With one swift bound the stag was up and away over the meadow, putting a great distance between himself and the fierce lion. He ran and ran until he came up to the wood and, without a second thought, he continued into the trees. But within moments he was caught fast by his great antlers in the branches of the tree and could not move at all. As the hungry lion bounded up, the vain stag realised that his despised thin legs had put him far beyond the clutches of the lion, but his antlers, of which he was so very proud, had eventually led to his downfall.

WHAT WE VALUE MOST IS NOT ALWAYS THAT WHICH IS OF MOST USE TO US.

The Wild Boar and the Fox

The fox was strolling through the forest, when he came upon a wild boar who appeared to be sharpening his tusks against a tree. The fox watched from a distance for he was aware that wild boar need to be treated with a certain amount of respect. But eventually his curiosity got the better of him and he crept closer. There was no doubt about it at all, the wild boar was definitely sharpening his tusks.

"Excuse me for asking, but can you tell me why you are sharpening your tusks?" enquired the fox very politely. "There are no hunters out today and I can see no other danger that would threaten such a beast as yourself."

The wild boar stopped what he was doing and looked at the fox. "True, my friend, but the hunters will be here again, and any other danger might threaten with no warning, then it would be too late for me to sharpen my tusks," and he went back to his task.

The fox nodded for he could see the sense of that and he continued on his way, thinking how very sensible the wild boar was.

DO NOT WAIT UNTIL DANGER IS UPON YOU BEFORE YOU MAKE YOUR PREPARATIONS.

The Dog and the Egg

The dog was so very fond of eggs that whenever he found one, he would gobble it up so fast that it barely touched the sides of his mouth. So when he chanced upon a bowl full of eggs waiting for the fisherman's lunch, he opened his mouth as wide as possible and in one great gulp swallowed one of the eggs. But it was not an egg. It was a clam and, of course, the shell was very hard. As the greedy dog had not taken the time to chew, the whole clam shell went down his throat and sat solidly in his stomach.

Needless to say, it was very heavy and the weight gave him great pain. "Serves me right," the dog grumbled to himself. "Obviously not everything round is an egg," and he went away, feeling very sorry for himself.

TAKE YOUR TIME BEFORE YOU ACT. THINGS ARE NOT ALWAYS WHAT THEY SEEM.

The Lion and the Frog

The lion was passing a pond one day, when he heard the sound of the frog croaking.

"Goodness me," he thought, "that must indeed be a mighty creature to make such a huge noise," and so he crept quietly closer to wait to see what animal was hiding, for he could see no one. The frog croaked again, and the puzzled lion slunk a little closer to the pond, but there was still no one to be seen. And then with another great "Croak!" the frog leapt onto a round stone at the water's edge.

"Goodness me!" exclaimed the lion crossly. "Have I been waiting all this time for such an insignificant creature?" and with one swipe of his great paw, the frog was gone.

BEWARE OF MAKING SO MUCH NOISE THAT YOU IGNORE IMMINENT DANGER.

The Fox and the Woodcutter

The woodcutter was just sharpening his axe, when the fox came running over the hill, breathing heavily with his tongue lolling out of his mouth.

"Please, good woodcutter, will you hide me? I am being chased by two huntsmen," the fox pleaded.

The woodcutter jerked his head towards his hut, and the grateful fox dashed inside and hid behind the door where he could see everything that was going on.

No sooner had the fox drawn breath, than the huntsmen were standing in front of the woodcutter.

"Good morning, woodcutter," said the huntsmen, "have you seen a fox pass this way?"

"No, I have not," replied the woodcutter, but to the fox's horror the woodcutter jerked his head towards the hut again.

But as the huntsmen were too busy looking all around for the fox, they missed the hint and so just thanked the woodcutter, then went on their way.

Once they were safely out of sight, the fox came out of the hut and started back the way he had originally come.

"Well, you might at least thank me for saving your skin," called out the sneaky woodcutter.

"Oh no," said the fox crossly, "you do not deserve my thanks. Your words did not match your actions, and I might be in the hunters' bag by now," and he walked away with a flick of his large bushy tail.

YOUR ACTIONS WILL ALWAYS SPEAK LOUDER THAN YOUR WORDS.

The Hunting Dog, the Lion and the Fox

A presumptuous hunting dog thought he would chase the lion who was just strolling by, so he bounded up after him. The lion, of course, was having none of this, so he turned round and roared a huge roar at the dog. The dog fled as fast as he could, his legs shaking in fright.

A fox, who had prudently hidden behind a tree when he saw the lion, called out to the dog, "Well that was very foolish, thinking you could take on the King of the Beasts," and he laughed at the terrified dog.

BEWARE OF CHALLENGING PEOPLE STRONGER THAN YOURSELF. IT WILL END IN SHAME.

The Ant and the Dove

The ant was very thirsty and so he crawled to the very edge of the stream to have a drink. But before he could even take a sip, a sudden swirl of water tipped him into the fast-flowing stream. It would all have been over for the tiny ant had not a kindly dove spotted his plight. She quickly dropped a stick into the water and the grateful ant was able to clamber up onto it and so to safety. The very next day, a hunter came by and set about making a cage of sticks to trap the dove. But the tiny ant saw what the hunter was about and quickly scuttled over and bit the hunter firmly on his ankle. With a yell of pain, the hunter dropped the sticks and the noise alerted the dove, who flew away, far from danger.

ONE GOOD TURN DESERVES ANOTHER.

The Fox and the Actor's Mask

The fox was roaming the streets looking for food and quietly slipped through an open door in his quest. Once inside the house, his keen nose could detect no delicious smells, alas, but he was utterly fascinated by what he did find. The house belonged to an actor and there was an amazing collection of things for the fox to rummage through. He found a great chest that was flung open. Its huge key was lying on the floor, together with some pages from a play. Many fine costumes spilt out, too, but what attracted the fox was a large white mask, which was clearly the work of a very fine craftsman. But when the fox took it up in his paws, it was just an empty shell.

The fox snorted in disgust. "A very fine head indeed, but it has no brains!" and he sloped off, looking once again for food.

BEWARE OF BEING TAKEN IN BY A HANDSOME FACE. THE PERSON BEHIND IT MAY BE VERY FOOLISH.

The Fox and the Grapes

A fox was passing a very tall tree that had a vine trained up its bark, when he spotted that there were several very fine bunches of grapes hanging high up. His mouth watering, the fox jumped as high as he could in a desperate bid to reach the grapes. But the harder he tried, the further off they seemed and eventually he realised he was never going to reach them. So he turned tail and, attempting to look very dignified, walked away, saying in a loud voice for anyone to hear, "I was foolish to imagine those grapes were worth eating. They are clearly quite sour."

DON'T BELITTLE THINGS THAT ARE BEYOND YOUR REACH OUT OF FRUSTRATION.

The Monkey as King

There was a great gathering of all the animals in the forest and the monkey entertained them greatly with his dancing. "Your dancing is very impressive," several of the animals cried. "You should become our king," they said, and so the foolish monkey put on the crown without a second thought and danced even more.

But the fox was disgusted with this as he did not consider the monkey at all worthy to be King of the Beasts, so when he spotted a trap set with a piece of meat, he went up to the monkey and said slyly, "I have found this delicious piece of meat, but instead of eating it myself, I thought that, as you are king, it would be only right and proper for you to have it instead." The monkey looked at the meat greedily without at all noticing that it was set in a trap, because, of course, he was not that bright. He reached out to snatch up the piece of meat, but he was immediately caught fast in the trap.

"Oh, wicked Fox," he cried, "you have led your king into great danger!"

But the fox only laughed.

"You call yourself King of the Beasts, pah! How could someone so foolish be king over us all?" and he stalked away, his nose in the air. Slowly all the other animals wandered off, too, leaving the monkey to reflect on his foolishness.

IF YOU DON'T THINK ABOUT YOUR ACTIONS CAREFULLY, YOU MIGHT MAKE A SERIOUS MISTAKE, AND GET LAUGHED AT INTO THE BARGAIN.

The Fox and the Monkey

The fox and the monkey fell into each other's company as they travelled along the road. Before too long, however, they were arguing fiercely as to which one of them came from the most noble family. They grew more and more cross with each other and their boasts grew more and more exaggerated. Now the road took them past a line of very fine tombs, and as they neared the end of the line, the monkey sighed and groaned deeply. "Whatever on earth is wrong?" asked the fox.

"How could you expect me to walk by the tombs of my great ancestors, all famous in their day, without showing my grief?" snapped the monkey.

"Ho ho," grinned the fox. "Very clever, my friend. You choose to magnify your lies by safely calling on the dead. None of these fellows could possibly rise up to contradict you!" And he walked away, leaving the boastful monkey spluttering with rage at being found out.

BEWARE OF PEOPLE WHO BOAST MOST WHEN THERE IS NO ONE AROUND WHO COULD CONTRADICT THEM.

The Fox without a Tail

A very handsome fox was unfortunate enough to get caught in a trap. After a great deal of struggling, he managed to get himself free, but only at the cost of his magnificent tail. He was so ashamed to be seen without his brush that he hid himself from his fellow foxes for many days. But then he came up with what he thought was a cunning plan. He would persuade all the other foxes to cut off their tails, so they would all look the same. So he called all the other foxes to a meeting and advised them to cut off their tails.

"They are so heavy to trail around with, and what possible use is a tail anyway?" he asked. But one of the foxes, who knew exactly just how useful his tail was, shouted out, "Look here, you are only giving us this advice because you don't want to be different. If you hadn't lost yours, you wouldn't be half as keen for the rest of us to cut ours off too!" And all the other foxes realised just how true this was, turned tail and walked off proudly.

DON'T LET PEOPLE PERSUADE YOU INTO DOING SOMETHING JUST BECAUSE IT SUITS THEIR NEEDS RATHER THAN YOURS.

The Lion, the Bear and the Fox

The great lion and the huge bear were fighting over a fawn they had found, as they both wanted to eat it for supper. The fight went on and on, and they were soon both exhausted and lying on the ground, gasping for breath. As they lay there helplessly, a wily fox came by and when he saw the fawn, he immediately snatched it up and ran away, thinking to himself, "Well here is a fine thing! I have defeated a great lion and a huge bear today to get my supper!"

The lion and the bear could only look on helplessly.

"What a ridiculous pair we are," gasped the lion.

"Indeed," groaned the bear, "we have both lost out on our supper."

BE CAREFUL OTHERS DO NOT BENEFIT FROM ALL YOUR HARD WORK WHILE YOU GAIN NOTHING.

The Lion, the Fox and the Donkey

The lion and the fox and the donkey made an agreement to go out hunting together. They were very successful and soon there was a very large catch to be divided between all three. The lion suggested to the donkey that he divide it out between the three of them. So the donkey did as he was bid and very carefully made three completely equal piles, and then invited the lion to choose his share. But the treacherous lion leapt on to the donkey and that was the end of her.

With a frown, the lion turned to the fox and said, "Now, Fox, please divide the pile between the two of us." The fox made one huge great pile, which he pushed towards the lion, and kept back a very small selection of morsels and said to the lion, "There you are, I have made my choice."

The lion smiled nastily. "Well done, Fox. How did you learn to share in such a satisfactory way?"

"I took a lesson from the donkey," said the fox sadly.

YOU CAN LEARN A GREAT DEAL OF WISDOM BY SEEING THE MISFORTUNES OF OTHERS.

The Ass, the Fox and the Lion

The foolish ass and the sneaky fox made an agreement to hunt together and then share whatever they managed to catch. All day long they stalked through the grass and round the stony outcrops, but they found nothing. Then, just as they had almost given up hope, they heard a rustling behind them. Turning round, they found to their horror it was a huge lion. The fox saw a way of saving his own skin and so went up to the lion very cautiously and whispered in his ear, "If you promise to let me go free, I can lead the ass to a trap further down the road and he will be all yours."

The lion agreed to this with a regal shake of his head, and so the fox led the poor ass down the pathway, pretending that the lion had agreed to let them both go. But as they came up to the hidden trap, the fox stepped to one side and the ass tumbled down into the trap, which was so deep he had no chance of getting out.

The fox was about to run off, when the lion bounded over to him and said, "Thank you for that, Fox. I shall enjoy the ass at my leisure, but first I will have you," and without further ado he did just that.

IF YOU BETRAY YOUR FRIENDS, YOU MAY WELL FIND YOURSELF IN EVEN MORE TROUBLE.

The Man and the Lion

The man and the lion had fallen into step with each other as they journeyed along the road. It was not long before they were trying to outdo each other by boasting about their strength and courage. As they trudged along the road, they came across a huge stone carving of a man strangling a lion.

"Ah well, there you see, my good lion, that we men are indeed stronger than lions," the man said triumphantly. "Doesn't this carving prove it to you?"

But the lion just smiled and said calmly, "That is a very simple view. Were lions able to carve, I can assure you that most statues would show the man lying underneath the lion!"

YOU MUST ALWAYS REMEMBER THAT THERE ARE TWO SIDES TO EVERY QUESTION.

The Lion, the Wolf and the Fox

A very old lion was lying in his den. He was sick and all the animals had come to visit the King of the Beasts - except the fox. The wolf saw this as a very good chance to pay off old scores with the fox and so he said to the lion, "I am sure you have noticed, O great Lord, that we have all come to pay our respects to you, all except the fox, that is."

Just at that moment, the fox came by the den in time to hear what the wolf was saying. He walked into the den boldly and right up to the lion, who roared at him in anger for his lack of respect. But the fox bowed deeply to the lion and asked to be allowed to explain himself.

"None of these animals cares for you half as much as I do," he proclaimed. "I have not been here because I have travelled far and spoken with many wise doctors, seeking a cure for your illness," he said.

"Well, may I know if you have found such a cure?" demanded the lion.

"Indeed I have," said the fox humbly. "You must catch a wolf while he is still alive and cut off his skin and then wrap yourself in it while it is still warm."

In a trice, with one swipe of his great paw, the wolf lay dead at the lion's feet and the other animals helped wrap the skin round his thin shoulders. The fox smiled smugly and went on his way.

BEWARE WHEN PLOTTING AGAINST ANOTHER THAT YOU DO NOT CAUSE YOUR OWN DOWNFALL.

The Wolf and the Lamb

The wolf came across the lamb all alone and drinking from the stream.

"Ah ha," the wolf thought, "my supper. But how can I justify taking this innocent beast?"

He thought a while and then called out to the lamb, "Lamb, you are muddying the water so I cannot drink."

But the lamb replied politely, "I don't think I am as I am drinking downstream from you, and anyway I only drink with the tip of my tongue."

The thwarted wolf thought for a moment and then said crossly, "Well last year you were very rude to me when I passed you in the meadow."

But once again the lamb replied very politely, "I was only born this spring, so I do not think it can have been me."

The wolf was very angry by this time and shouted across the stream, "Well you have been eating the grass in my pasture."

The lamb was still very polite in his response. "I have not tasted grass yet," he replied.

"Enough excuses!" yelled the wolf. "I am not going to go without my supper," and he leapt across the stream and that was the end of the poor innocent lamb.

IF AN ENEMY HAS DECIDED TO DO YOU WRONG, HE WILL IGNORE ANY PLEA NO MATTER HOW JUST.

The Wolf and the Lion

The wolf was running for shelter with a sheep he had just stolen, when he met a lion. The lion, of course, grabbed the sheep from the wolf and walked on by. There was little the wolf could do against the huge beast, but once the lion was some distance away, he called out after him, with a quaver in his voice, "That sheep is my property, you have no right to take her away."

The lion just laughed. "Your property, eh? I imagine it was a present from a friend!" and he continued on his way, the sheep still firmly in his grasp.

ONE THIEF WILL TURN AGAINST ANOTHER, IF THEY ARE BOTH OUT OF LUCK.

The Goatherd and the Wild Goats

High up on the mountain pasture, the goatherd was tending his flock, when he noticed that several wild goats had come down the mountainside and mingled with his herd.

As dusk began to fall, the goatherd rounded up all the goats together, his own and the wild ones, and drove them down to his hut - where he put them all together in the pen.

The next day the weather was so stormy that the goatherd was unable to let the goats out, so he had to feed them in the pen. He very carefully gave all his own animals just enough to keep them from being famished, but he was very generous in the portions he gave to the wild goats, for he thought this would make them stay with him and so he would increase his flock.

The next day the weather was still wild and windy, so once again the goatherd gave the wild goats much more to eat than his own herd.

When he awoke the next morning, the sun was shining, so he drove all the goats - the wild ones and his own herd - out of the pen and high up onto the mountain pasture. No sooner had they reached the pasture than all the wild goats ran away as fast as possible.

The goatherd was really cross and ran after them, calling out, "Why are you so ungrateful? Surely I have treated you really well?"

One of the wild goats turned round and spoke to the goatherd. "Yes indeed, you did treat us very well, too well in fact. That is what makes us run away now."

The goatherd muttered, "But that doesn't make sense. How could I treat you too well?"

"Quite simple," replied the wild goat. "If you treat us as newcomers better than your own flock, what happens when you find another herd of wild goats? You will surely treat them better than us!" and he kicked up his heels and ran away to join all the other wild goats.

MAKE NEW FRIENDS BUT REMEMBER TO KEEP THE OLD.

The Tame Ass and the Wild Ass

A wild ass was trotting down a steep path, when he saw a tame ass sitting peacefully in the sun, eating from an overflowing manger of hay.

"My, you are a lucky fellow," said the wild ass. "There you are, looking all sleek and content, and here I am having to look for every last mouthful of food."

The tame ass said nothing, but continued to munch contentedly at his hay.

But the very next day, as the wild ass was trotting along the path, he met the tame ass again and this time he was carrying a huge load of wood in two baskets across his back. Behind him walked a man with a great stick, who was shouting at the tame ass to walk faster.

"Ah, my friend," said the wild ass, "I see now that you pay very dearly for your comfort and having plenty to eat," and he walked away, grateful for his freedom.

IF YOU HAVE TO PAY DEARLY FOR YOUR ADVANTAGES, THEN IT IS DOUBTFUL IF THEY ARE A REAL BLESSING.

The Ass Carrying the Statue

The ass was being driven into town to the temple, with a great statue of a god on his back. Before too long, he noticed that everyone was taking off their hats and bowing as he passed by. Now the foolish ass imagined that the people were bowing out of respect for himself and his head began to swell with conceit. "Why should I be forced to carry on like this, if I am so important?" he thought to himself, and so he dug in his heels, let out a great bray and refused to take another step. His driver at first could not make out what was making the ass behave in such a way, but when he realised what the problem was, he hit him very hard with his stick and yelled at him, "You vain and stupid ass, do you really think the people are worshipping you, a mere ass? Be on your way at once!"

BEWARE OF MAKING YOURSELF LOOK FOOLISH BY TAKING CREDIT THAT IS RIGHTLY DUE TO OTHERS.

The Ass and the Wolf

The ass was feeding peacefully in the meadow, when he saw his enemy the wolf creeping towards him. The clever ass pretended to be lame and hobbled painfully up to the wolf.

"Dear Ass," smiled the wolf slyly, "I am troubled to see you so clearly in pain. What has caused this?"

"I stepped on a thorn when I was jumping through a hedge," replied the ass. "I would ask you to remove the thorn, otherwise when you eat me, the thorn could stick in your throat and hurt you."

So the wolf lifted up the ass's foot and began to examine it closely, looking for the thorn. The ass suddenly gave the wolf a mighty kick in the mouth and knocked out all his teeth. Then he galloped away, for there was nothing wrong with his foot. The wolf was left, spitting out broken teeth, and muttering to himself, "I should have listened to my father who taught me to be a butcher, not a doctor."

IF YOU INTERFERE WITH THINGS THAT DO NOT CONCERN YOU, YOU MUST EXPECT TO GET INTO TROUBLE.

The Dog and the Wolf

The dog was dozing in the sun in front of his master's house when the great wolf pounced on him. He was just about to eat him, when the dog cried out, "Wait, wait, Wolf! Look how skinny I am, there is hardly a scrap of flesh on my bones. I would make a poor meal."

The wolf paused and the dog wriggled back to his feet. "Now, Wolf, if you come back in a few days, my master is going to give a great feast," the dog explained. "There will be many rich pickings for me, and I shall be considerably fatter and much more tasty, if only you would wait until then."

So the wolf bounded off, congratulating himself on such a very good arrangement. When he came back in a few days' time, the dog was dozing in the sun again, but this time he was on the roof of his master's house.

"Dog, you must come down and keep to our arrangement," called the wolf.

"My foolish Wolf, if you ever catch me lying down on the ground again, don't wait for the feast," replied the dog with a wide smile, and the hungry wolf just slunk away, greatly regretting his stupidity.

IF ONCE YOU ARE CAUGHT OUT, YOU SHOULD NEVER MAKE THE SAME MISTAKE AGAIN.

The Dog and the Shadow

The dog was crossing the river with a piece of meat in his mouth, when suddenly he noticed his own reflection in the still water. Stupidly thinking it was another dog with an even bigger piece of meat in his mouth, the dog dropped his own piece of meat. He sprang into the water to attack the other dog and steal the bigger piece. Of course there was no other dog, so in the end the dog lost his own piece of meat and was very wet into the bargain.

IF YOU ALWAYS DESIRE MORE THAN YOU HAVE, YOU MAY WELL END UP WITH NOTHING.

The Pig and the Sheep

The pig found her way into a meadow where the sheep were grazing quietly and, finding it to her liking, she stayed there for some time. But one day, the shepherd came up behind the pig and went to grab her, intending to take her to the butcher. The pig squealed and struggled to get free. The sheep looked on in astonishment. "Why are you making such a noise?" they cried. "The shepherd catches us regularly, but we don't make such a fuss."

"Yes, but it is quite different for you," retorted the pig, still struggling to get away from the shepherd. "All he wants from you is your wool, you silly creatures. He wants me for bacon!"

IF IT IS YOUR LIFE THAT IS IN DANGER, YOU WILL SHOUT LOUDER THAN IF IT IS JUST YOUR PROPERTY.

The Fox and the Cicada

The cicada was chirping in the branches of a tall tree, when the fox heard her as he was passing by.

"Ah, now that cicada would make a tasty start to my supper," he thought to himself. "I shall have to entice her down where I can catch her."

So the fox looked up into the tree with his most winning smile and sang her praises in the most extravagant terms.

"Dear Cicada, you have such a glorious voice," he said. "Please do come down, so I can meet you in person."

But the cicada did not trust the fox, so she sent a leaf whirling down to the ground. The fox pounced on it immediately, convinced it was the cicada.

"So my friend, you say you would like to meet me to praise my voice?" the cicada called down to the fox. "Why then were you so quick to leap on that leaf? Perhaps you thought it was me?"

"Not at all, dear lady," the fox blustered. "I was only tidying the leaf away."

But the cicada knew better. "I have seen too many cicada wings lying outside fox dens to be fooled by you," she replied.

So the fox just had to slink away, still hungry.

IF YOU ARE WISE, YOU WILL LEARN FROM THE MISFORTUNES OF OTHERS.

The Gnat and the Bull

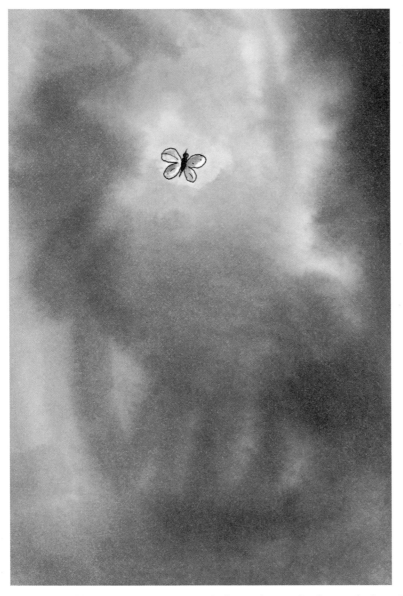

The gnat was really tired as he had been flying all day, so he was delighted when he spied a large bull in a field. The gnat alighted on the bull's horn and stayed there for a considerable time without moving. When he was rested and was about to fly away again, he said to the bull, "I do hope I haven't inconvenienced you, and if it is all right with you, now that I am rested, I should like to fly away again."

The bull barely moved his head, but lifted his eyes to look at the presumptuous gnat. "I didn't even notice your arrival, so I am sure your departure will be of no consequence to me either," he said, and he carried on snoozing.

BEWARE OF THINKING THAT YOU ARE MORE IMPORTANT THAN YOU REALLY ARE.

The Lion, Jupiter and the Elephant

The lion was a mighty beast of great strength, with sharp teeth and claws, and yet he could not bear the sound of a cock crowing and would always run away whenever he heard one. He was very ashamed of this one weakness, and complained endlessly to Jupiter for making him thus. But Jupiter had no sympathy for the lion.

"I have given you everything I possibly could: great strength and the ability to defend yourself with your sharp teeth and claws," he reasoned. "If this is your only failing, you should be well content." But the lion would not be comforted and could not bear to be such a coward, so much so that he wished he might die.

It was in this state of mind that he met up with the elephant. They talked for a long time, and the lion couldn't help noticing that the elephant kept flapping his great big ears about all the time. Eventually, he just had to ask, "Whatever is the matter, elephant? Why do you keep flapping your ears about so?"

The elephant replied in a quavery voice, "Do you see that irritating little insect buzzing around my head? If he gets into my ear then I am done for, so I am terrified of him."

The lion was astonished and immediately abandoned all thoughts of dying.

"If the huge elephant is so distressed by such a tiny thing as an insect, then why should I be embarrassed by being afraid of a cock, which is so much bigger than an insect?" he told himself, and forthwith he stopped pestering Jupiter so endlessly.

OTHER PEOPLE MAY HAVE GREATER FEARS THAN YOUR OWN.

The Dog, the Cock and the Fox

The dog and the cock became very good friends and agreed that they would travel together. They were quite far from home when they decided to rest for the night, so they found a tall tree with a hollow at the base of the trunk. The cock flew up into the branches of the tree and the dog curled up in the hollow, and they both passed a very peaceful night.

Just as dawn came the following morning, the cock awoke and, as usual, crowed loudly to announce the new day. The fox was passing by and immediately thought to make the cock his breakfast, so he sidled up to the tree and called up to the cock, "I should very much like to meet the owner of this splendid voice. Please do come down the tree."

The cock replied sweetly, "Of course, dear Fox. If you wake up the porter who is sleeping down below, he will certainly let you in."

So the unwary fox went round to the hollow at the bottom of the tree and, peering into the dark of the hole, said importantly, "Ho there, Porter! Open up immediately as I wish to meet with the glorious voiced Cock!"

But, of course, the wise dog knew exactly what the fox was up to and so he leapt out, and that was the end of the fox!

WHEN YOU ARE IN DANGER, REMEMBER HOW MUCH YOUR REAL FRIENDS CAN HELP YOU.

The Ass and the Shepherd

The shepherd was sitting in a meadow with his ass who was grazing peacefully nearby. The shepherd thought he could hear the sound of shouting in the distance and, when he turned and looked over his shoulder, to his horror he saw a great troop of enemy soldiers coming over the bridge.

"Quick, Ass, we must flee immediately or we will be captured by those fierce looking soldiers, and then goodness knows what will happen to us!" he shouted, and tried to get the ass to follow as he began to run away. But the ass was in no hurry to move.

"Do you think I will be made to carry heavier loads than I have with you, if I am captured?" he asked the shepherd lazily.

"I don't think so at all," said the shepherd, who had always made the ass work extremely hard indeed.

"Then why should I exert myself to run away when I won't be any worse off?" said the ass calmly, and he continued to graze as though he didn't have a care in the world.

ONE MASTER MAY BE JUST AS GOOD AS ANOTHER.

The Hare and the Hound

The hound chased a hare out from her hiding place and although he ran as fast as possible, she was able to get away from him. So the hound gave up and wandered back to where a goatherd was sitting, watching his flock.

The goatherd laughed at the hound. "Well, she was too fast for you, even though she was so much smaller!"

But the hound was not going to be humiliated in this way. "She was running to save her life. I was running to catch my next meal," he retorted.

BEWARE OF THOSE WHO ALWAYS HAVE A CLEVER ANSWER TO COVER THEIR OWN INADEQUACY.

ABOUT AESOP

Although Aesop's fables are very familiar, few people know much about the man himself. Most of what has been written about Aesop was recorded long after his death and so needs to be treated with a certain amount of caution. He is supposed to have lived from around 620 to 560BCE. Even his birthplace is not known for sure - it might have been Thrace or Samos or even Athens. We do know that he was a slave who was freed by his owner and in all probability he met his death violently at the hands of the people of Delphi. He is often depicted as being very ugly, but a statue of him carved by the famous sculptor Lysippus, some two hundred years after his death, shows a man of great nobility. The first recorded mention of his life came from Aristotle, and his account was followed by the Greek historian Herodotus, who called Aesop "a writer of fables".

Aesop is very unlikely to have written down his fables himself, but he would have recited them at public gatherings. The first written collection is supposed to have appeared around 320BCE. This disappeared and it wasn't until Phaedrus, a former slave himself, translated them into Latin in the first century CE that a lasting version was created. There were many versions thereafter and they became very well known in medieval Europe. Eventually William Caxton translated a German edition, which then became one of the first books ever printed in the English language. It is quite possible that the fables we are now all very familiar with bear little resemblance to the originals as told by Aesop. However, they are known throughout the Western world as Aesop's fables and their wisdom is uncontested.

FULVIO TESTA is one of Italy's most distinguished artists and illustrators and has had many exhibitions in the United States and Europe. In addition to his own prize-winning books, he has illustrated titles by authors such as Anthony Burgess and Gianni Rodari.

FIONA WATERS was born in Edinburgh, and is famous in the children's book world for her passion and enthusiasm. She has written over eighty children's books, and won the CLPE Poetry Prize in 2007.